WHAT BOOKS PRESS

AN IMPRINT OF

THE GLASS TABLE

COLLECTIVE

LOS ANGELES

THE SHORTEST FAREWELLS ARE THE BEST

FLASH NOIR FICTION

CHUCK ROSENTHAL

&

GAIL WRONSKY

LOS ANGELES

Publisher's Cataloging-In-Publication Data
Rosenthal, Chuck, 1951-
    The shortest farewells are the best : flash noir fiction / Chuck Rosenthal & Gail Wronsky.
      pages ; cm
    ISBN: 978-0-9962276-2-9
    1. Film noir--Fiction. 2. Noir fiction, American. 3. Short stories, American. I. Wronsky, Gail. II. Title.
PS3568.O8368 S56 2015
813/.54

Cover art: Gronk, *fragment night*, acrylic on canvas, 2013
Book design by Ash Goodwin, ashgood.com

What Books Press
363 South Topanga Canyon Boulevard
Topanga, CA 90290

WHATBOOKSPRESS.COM

THE SHORTEST
FAREWELLS ARE THE BEST

CONTENTS

"The cheaper the crook, the gaudier the patter."

—Sam Spade (Humphrey Bogart) in THE MALTESE FALCON

How could I have known that murder could sometimes smell like honeysuckle. Guys like him don't get that way overnight, do they? There's a speed limit in this state. I guess I'm in love with you. Looks like we're closed for the rest of the afternoon.

I DON'T CARE WHAT
YOUR SECRETS ARE

You're not connected with the automobile club, are you? You're too slick for your own good. I killed him for money, for a woman. Their perfume has the rotten sweetness of corruption. I didn't get the money and I didn't get the woman. What I didn't know was that she had plans of her own. I sent her a telegram begging her to come home. I don't get your game here. Who do you think I shot? What's the matter? Aren't you going to kiss me?

EVERYBODY HAS SOMETHING TO CONCEAL

13

Down there you work on one track and live on another. My sleep is so near waking that it's hardly worth the name. You've got a dead man lying at your feet—how did it happen? By the way, what stiff did you get that suit off? You're not very tall, are you. What does the law say about this kind of murder? Suppose I have to rap you over the knuckles? I'd feel better about it if you'd have a drink with me. But the man with the gun won't let me. How much do you remember about last night?

HE KILLED AND HE DESERVED
TO BE KILLED

Such a lot of guns around town and so few brains. I haven't lived a good life—
I've been bad. I don't mind a reasonable amount of trouble. I like to see people
drink. It was an accident. He pulled the gun. You shudder at the touch of my
hands as if they were the hands of death. You could lose teeth talking like that.
Do you think it's safe to leave me alone in this delirious state of mind? Now get
out of here before I throw my desk at you.

YOU'RE MADE TO ORDER
FOR THE RAP

15

Stop talking about Saturday night. Try telling me the facts. We never arrest a
man just for knowing where the body was. I like cheap perfume. It don't last
long but it hits harder. It's a lie. It's a lie. It's a lie! And I knew what he was
going to do. For every move, he threw a shadow. I don't think dancing is such
a good idea. Just what is it you're afraid of? I've got two boys outside in the car.
Be a good girl and give me another minute. It's only blackmail, baby, when
you're dumb enough to get caught. They won't be looking for a brunette.

PRETTY SONG—TOO BAD IT WAS
THE BACKGROUND TO MURDER

In the heat of action men are likely to forget where their passions take them.
They're not the first pair of women's shoes I've found in front of that couch.
That's what I'm paid for, not finding dead bodies. One thing I can't stand is
a guy trying to put something over on me. Give me a drink. I could use it.
Now lock that gun in the suitcase and throw the key away. Saving your kisses
for your husband? I'm in love with the back of your neck. I've always been
a liar. The trouble with you is you can't take it.

DEATH ALWAYS COMES AS
SORT OF AN ACCIDENT

I like smart women, they've got cat in them. How come you're holding out on me, baby? With that kind of figure you could get any man in the place. I brought you something from Tokyo. Still want to marry me? What's the matter—think I live under a rock or something? Don't tell me he's under the sofa too. I don't know anything about women. Suppose you tell me about it from the very beginning.

HE'S DONE THINGS TO ME
I CAN'T EVEN TALK ABOUT

He was mean when he was drunk. It isn't so easy for a girl—drifting around from one job to another. Most women are unhappy. They just pretend they aren't. I was lonely. I couldn't stand my loneliness. It was I you intended to kill, wasn't it? The funny part is it made a great deal of difference. You never knew me. You never bothered to figure me out. Like you said, we better call it quits. You killed my husband, Sam. You couldn't plant enough flowers around here to kill the stench. What was your wife like?

YOU NEVER FOOLED ME WITH YOUR SONG AND DANCE

You didn't kill him. You tried and you didn't. It's business, same as any
other business, except instead of price cutting it's throat cutting. Nothing
comes to you, nothing except death. Sounds like a nice ordinary life, doesn't
it? Listen, stop, stop minding other people's business if you want to stay
alive. Do you know what business I'm in? I'm from homicide. I came about
a murder. There's lipstick on that cup. The trouble with you, baby, is you
have no imagination.

What am I gonna do, take back that knife I put in that guy? The truth is, I'm in a jam. I'm ruined. My whole life. I'm drunk and I got no job. I have a terrible, terrible confession to make. Murder can be a chain, one link leading to another until it encircles your neck. The only type of killing that's safe is when a stranger kills a stranger—no motive—nothing to link the victim to the executioner. I don't want to get my name in the newspaper. Do you? Everybody makes mistakes, the wrong job, the wrong marriage. Prisons are bulging with prisoners who wonder how they got there. You knew what was goin on, so don't go gettin holy on me.

YOU DON'T LOOK TO ME LIKE
A MAN USED TO WHISTLING

What's the use of trying to tell you anything. If I had any sense I'd walk out
on you. You don't know how tough it was in there.   It didn't bother you when
I was in your arms. I told you not to call me here. One word from me and
you're out of business. I expect you to use your brains. You saw the cigarette
burns on her body.

SHE WAS JUST A FLASHY BLONDE
PUTTING ON AN ACT

Do you suppose she could have killed him? When the dice roll, you've gotta take what comes. You've got to shower and get some cocktails ready. I suppose you could call this a confession when you hear it. If you've got another suit, don't bother to unpack.

LUCKY GIRL—LIVING A LIFE OF PASSION AND VIOLENCE

23

The living room was still stuffy from last night's cigars. The drinks? Polynesian pearl-divers. And don't spare the rum. I'm gonna drink mine and have a sip of yours, that'll be something different for a change. When I found him he was dead. I didn't know he was hurt bad. I didn't know he was gonna die. I won't be sent back to that dime-a-dance joint—not if I can help it. If you killed anyone I'd feel responsible. You shouldn't fool around with a married woman. It's not a matter of sex, it's a matter of money. If you've been listening, just forget what you heard. Maybe someday I can do you a real favor.

SHE'S A YOUNG GIRL—YOU SHOULDN'T LET HER DRINK SO MUCH

I don't like you. I don't like the way you talk and I don't like your friends.
I wouldn't give two cents for a dame without a temper. That's what I wanted
most, I guess, somebody decent. The whole thing's wrong from the beginning.
I just can't believe it—you, a killer. I don't know how much you love him.
but even prison is better than death. At least you got a nice clean ambulance.
It's more than some of us get.

WHEN WE'RE YOUNG WE HAVE DREAMS THAT NEVER PAN OUT

Keep asking for it and you're gonna get it. Things are rough all over.
Simmer down, you'll live longer. If he dies, I'll tell you one thing—I'll kill
you. Love. Who gets love? It's all in the cards. I don't like guns. It's tough
to kill somebody who's not dependable. It would make our disappointment
so much worse.

She talks to me just once, and like that, she's dead. Do you look down on all women or just the ones you know? What do these look like, grapefruit? I'm not married. I have no designs on you. And one drink will do it. This is some conversation we're having. Now I'm supposed to know what I'm talking about. Give him a drink. You heard me, give him a drink. I'm glad we're getting close to something. It's much better to have looks than brains, cuz most men I know can see better than they can think.

27

I don't care who loves who, I won't play the sap for it. I had a feeling I could go for her. I like people to like me. Now when it's quiet I get nervous. How about a little rum to get this up on its feet? Everybody has a first drink, don't they? But they don't have to become a lush. You don't think I had anything to do with it. Now it doesn't matter. It doesn't matter at all. I'm not such a bad guy, you know.

It was his story against mine, but of course I told my story better. I like
dice and I like talking. I like women. And I don't like cops. That's right, I
want more. Everybody thinks they live forever, that's a laugh, but they don't.
Sometimes I feel like I don't know what it's all about anymore. Look at him
lying here; ain't much now, is he? When barflies get killed, there's any number
of crummy reasons. You don't remember firing the gun? Don't brag about it.
How about a pair of alligator shoes with my compliments.

WHAT'S YOUR STORY

29

I come from a family that does things. I seem to exist largely on heat, like a
newborn spider. I was finally getting in with the real boys. You were in one
of those moods that keep me awake all night. You can't buck the system,
Eddie. You'll never get anywhere in this town not liking thieves. Look it up
in the papers—she was murdered last night. Yeah—dead. It was the act of
a sick man with an urge to destroy. Sometimes people are where they can't
talk—under six feet of dirt maybe. The rat fell out of his chair and we just
left him there. I don't know what I was doing in the same room with him.
Tell that to your mother.

MEN, WITH EYES LIKE MARBLES, THEY WATCH

When it comes to picking the killer, you've picked the wrong guy. You figure I've got a gun so you can't trust me. Try to look at me when you're talking. You know, I almost killed her an hour ago. I should've. I got plans—see? There's no room in em for you. Knock off the nuts and dumb stuff. You have a little trouble with perspective. Private lessons will fix that. The shortest farewells are the best. Do all your friends carry ice-picks?

YOU LOOK LIKE
A QUIET AFTERNOON AT THE
TEAHOUSE OF THE RISING MOON

Do you always go around leaving your fingerprints on a girl's shoulder? Not that I mind particularly. You've got nice strong hands. And then she walked in out of the moonlight, smiling. And for months afterwards, corpses were found in the mangrove swamps.

YOU GIVE ME ANY TROUBLE AND
I'LL FILL YOU FULL OF LEAD

You killed him—that ought to satisfy you. You're no good for anyone but me. Yes, angel, they're going to send you over. I don't want any part of that cage. Let's get out of this lobster trap and get some salt air. You've been a lot of places, haven't you. Every time I look at the sky I think of all the places I've never been. I'm kind of sensitive myself. We weren't meant to be happy. I haven't had a good laugh since Johnny was murdered.

NO GUNS, NO COPS,
NO TRUCKS

33

Say, I like this—early nothing. Where have we met—in another guy's dream?
I remember he said goodbye. I think he was crying. I'm not used to having
my head in the clouds. It was the walk of a dead man. We don't talk about
those kinds of things around here. Did you watch his face? Maybe this is the
face that'll haunt you. Maybe these are the eyes that'll drive you crazy.

EVERY TIME WE GET TOGETHER
THERE'S NOTHING BUT TROUBLE

You think I like meeting you like this? If he finds out about us he'll kill me.
What good is money or business to a dead man. Try talking and find out.
I was beginning to think you worked in bed, like Marcel Proust. A man who
can't see that hasn't got eyes. You sure you don't see what you hear? You're like
a leaf the wind blows from one gutter to another. Well, if it isn't the laundry
man himself. Looks like a sex crime to me. I'll take that cigarette now.

MURDER NEVER SOLVES ANYTHING

35

His own mother wouldn't know him. He was as crisp as bacon. I'm not drunk, I'm cold sober. I need a drink. Let's go down to the bar, we can cool off while we try to impress each other. Whoever was on that roof is still loose. Obviously, killing has a fascination for him. I knew he'd come to a bad end. When it comes, it won't be quick and it won't be pretty. What do you know about me? What do they want from you? Why are they pointing those guns at us?

I'D DO ANYTHING TO SAVE
MY HUSBAND, ANYTHING

Since he was dead, I was glad of it. What was left of the day was like a pack of cigarettes you smoked. It's funny, too, how a kiss stays on—how you can taste it. If he was mean or vicious I'd have liked him better. I'm not scared and you know it. You can't do a thing to me, not a thing. You say you loved her in the same breath you say you killed her. You don't love me. You make me homesick for some of the worst years of my life. I guess I'm in love with you. Nothing ever happens to me, you know that. Nothing in the world is any good unless you can share it. I know lotsa Larrys. This is hopeless.

HOW DO YOU WANT ME TO TELL YOUR STORY?

37

Buddy, you look like you're in trouble. Everybody wants to read about the murder. You mind telling me what happened? He brought me down to headquarters. Cops are paid to take risks. I'm not. Each one is a horrible killer. But all they want is a quick confession. Is it difficult to kill a man? Answer me straight or I'll blow your head off—where are the bodies?

I STILL ENJOY THE SMELL OF IT

I used to sit there half-asleep with the beer and the darkness. What to do in a wind of night-blooming jasmine but wait and sweat. Sometimes an ill wind is like a bad memory. Sitting here thinking's kind of rough when you've spent your life not thinking. You're looking, sir, at a very dull survival of a very gaudy life. It was all in the cards and there was no way of stopping it. I also know what I don't want and I don't want to be rushed. Everything turns cold inside me. I don't like the word confession. You little phony. Put pistons in your eyes and keep your voice low. Nothing's going to happen. I swear to you, nothing's going to happen. The last stop is the cemetery.

Anybody follow you? I didn't know homicide guys hung out in the morgue. Died three days ago. Bad ticker. I figured you slugged her with that ashtray because she gave you trouble. I took you back when you came whimpering and crawling. I should've kicked your teeth in. How stupid can you get. All she wanted was to save her own dirty neck. I gave all that to missing persons. And then somehow there I was. You got no idea how lonely it gets. It didn't work out. What a pity it didn't work out. Everything's coming out of Kansas City now. To me it's the end of the brightness of life.

YOU KNOW WOMEN—
THE STUBBORN SEX

Good times, that's what I want. I once kissed a guy and stabbed him in the back at the same time. There was something about the big lug I didn't like. There's nothing like a love song to give you a good laugh. Let's dance. You're my best customer. You wanna lay a price on that? What about a nice bottle of wine to celebrate? I guess I'm not much of a woman. I probably looked dumb to you when you slugged me, but I'm not dumb. You like working girls over, don't you. I didn't get married to sleep alone. I found another guy—a real doll. Roulette wheels have a way of running over me. Is it beneath your dignity to ask directions?

HE KNOWS HIS LIFE ISN'T WORTH
A PLUG NICKEL

41

Do you know what Johnny Dillinger said about guys like you? He said you were just rushin toward death—rushin toward death. You ought to take it easy on that liquor. She's gonna throw an awful fit when she finds out what kind of guy you are. I ain't sore at nobody. I'm just sayin what I see. There must be someplace we can go. And I didn't say anything, remember?

YOU BEGIN TO INTEREST ME, VAGUELY

You want to knock him off, don't you. They call it killer amnesia. Once a crook, always a crook. Once a tramp, always a tramp. You wanna talk business or do you wanna play house? If you tell the truth nobody believes you. Tell me about paradise and all the things I'm missing. He's getting that look in his eye. Always worries me when these hoodlums get religion. You must act naturally— smile at them. Somewhere, someone will crack. I'll leave the door unlocked, you can walk in anytime. See what I mean, hurricanes yet.

Don't worry, there'll be a payoff. Fog seems to be lifting. Let's go out there and climb a couple of mountains. It's practically the middle of the night. What do you do—go on singing songs and drinking Ramos gin fizzes? All these big emotions are wonderful, but they just kind of scare me. Lady, there was a time I coulda used you. Trouble is, you always know what you want. You gotta leave him sometime so why not leave him now? We'll have dinner tonight— but not together. Maybe if I was a little bit smart I'd be a little bit lucky. The dumbest thing you did was kill Pete. It was in the cards; it was fate. You don't even know what I'm talking about.

BABY, I DON'T CARE

Would you like a smoke now? It sort of lightens my chores. It wasn't an accident. She was murdered. He said something went wrong. It certainly did. I never saw anyone so afraid to die. The smell of music in her hair. After the killing everything was quiet. No nerves, not a tear, not even a blink of the eyes. I never wanted to be tied down to anything or anybody in my life. They'll always be looking for us—they won't stop until we die. Would you like a smoke now?

DAMES—YOU'VE HEARD OF THEM, HAVEN'T YOU?

"I came down here to ask you to keep my name out of the papers."

"I never put anything down on paper."

"I have no feelings for you. I'm annoyed whenever I see you."

"Is there anything else you didn't tell me?"

"I meant it—I thought you was dead."

"I'm sorry I lost my temper. Don't wait up for me."

"How long should I keep up this uncongenial bar life?"

"How many men can a bullet kill?"

"Is that any of your business? Now I wonder how you don't get into trouble."

"Would it make any sense if I told you this never happened before?"

"If only we'd met long ago."

"Go on, shoot. Shoot!"

"I'm enjoying it more already."

I'd like to see you get plastered some night and drive off a cliff. There's no sacrifice too great for a chance at immortality. You've decided people are all scared rabbits and you spit on them. Don't get me wrong. I'm not a tough guy—just careful. You're the boss. You've got everybody over a barrel. Back away, you two-bit chiseler. Look, I'm trying to give you a chance. Maybe you better start drinking again.

He buy you that coat? Tell him he's a lucky man. You were drunk, you don't know what happened. I wasn't sore for him, or sore at her. I wasn't anything. You were the inside man. I'm going to spread the word that you talked. You scum. You get your news fast, dontcha? Why did you come back? Keep the motor running and the headlights on. Burn that tent you're wearing and get yourself a suit. I'm sorry, you'll all have to go. It's been a perfectly hideous party. You boys ever killed anybody?

ACKNOWLEDGMENTS

Every line in these flash fictions was taken from one of the following
40's and 50's noir films:

Breaking Point
City of Fear
Criss Cross
Dark Passage
Dead Reckoning
Desperate
Double Indemnity
High Sierra
Human Desire
In a Lonely Place
Jeopardy
Johnny Eager
Key Largo
Notorious

Out of the Past
Pushover
Scarlett Street
The Big Heat
The Big Sleep
The Blue Gardenia
The Brothers Rico
The Enforcer
The Maltese Falcon
The Postman Always Rings Twice
The Stranger
The Woman in the Window
Tomorrow Is Another Day
White Heat

Most of the pieces in this book were originally published in *Intellectual Refuge*.
The authors wish to express their gratitude to Christopher Schnieders,
Editor in Chief.

CHUCK ROSENTHAL is the author of twelve previous books and numerous stories and essays. *The Shortest Farewells Are the Best* is his second collaboration with Gail Wronsky, the first being *Tomorrow You'll Be One of Us*, a book of sci-fi poems illustrated by Gronk. He lives with Gail Wronsky in Topanga Canyon, California.

GAIL WRONSKY is the author of eleven books of poetry, prose, and translations, several of them collaborative. Her poems have appeared in *Poetry*, *Pool*, *Volt*, *Denver Quarterly*, *Boston Review*, and other literary magazines. She teaches poetry and women's literature at Loyola Marymount University, Los Angeles.

WHAT BOOKS PRESS

LOS ANGELES

TITLES FROM
WHAT BOOKS PRESS

POETRY

Molly Bendall & Gail Wronsky, *Bling & Fringe (The L.A. Poems)*

Laurie Blauner, *It Looks Worse Than I Am*

Kevin Cantwell, *One of Those Russian Novels*

Ramón García, *Other Countries*

Karen Kevorkian, *Lizard Dream*

Patty Seyburn, *Perfecta*

Judith Taylor, *Sex Libris*

Lynne Thompson, *Start with a Small Guitar*

Gail Wronsky, *So Quick Bright Things*
BILINGUAL, SPANISH TRANSLATED BY ALICIA PARTNOY

ART

Gronk, *A Giant Claw*
BILINGUAL, SPANISH

Chuck Rosenthal, Gail Wronsky & Gronk,
Tomorrow You'll Be One of Us: Sci Fi Poems